A Multitude of Sins

The Abigail Baker
Mystery Series Book 2

By Mary B. Barbee

Editing Team: Jenny Raith and Molly Misko

Cover design by Daniela Colleo of www.stunningbookcovers.com/

www.marybbarbee.com

For Father Pat, who heard my sins when
I received the Sacrament of Reconciliation as a child.

"Above all, love each other deeply, because love covers over a multitude of sins."

1 Peter 4:8

Chapter One

The alluring scent of bacon frying in the pan hung in the air as Jeremiah Baker entered the kitchen. His curly black hair was tamed and smoothed, parted on the side. His long beard was trimmed and neat. A crisp white cotton shirt and black pants were his everyday uniform, pressed neatly with creases purposefully placed where they belong.

Abigail Baker stood at the range, using a fork to turn the bacon. Her dark curls were less tamed but pulled back into a bun. Three thin spiral curls had found their way out of her hair tie and pins, perfectly framing her pretty face. Before she left the house she would be sure to tuck her curls under a *kapp*, but she had overslept and woke in a rush to prepare breakfast for the family. She had yet to finish getting ready for the day herself. There would be time for that after everyone else was out the door. Her plain dark blue dress hung long and brushed her bare ankles as she walked to greet her husband with a kiss.

"You look nice, today, *lieb*," she said, as she lowered back down from her tippy toes, her arms lingering around her husband's shoulders. Jeremiah was a tall man, standing just over six feet, a head taller than his wife.

"*Denki*," Jeremiah responded with a smile. "Same to you. You always look very nice," he said, caressing Abigail's cheek with a gentle stroke of the back of his hand.

Abigail smiled graciously and returned to the stovetop to remove the cooked bacon from the grease, setting it on a paper towel. Angel, the family's golden retriever, sat at her feet wearing her cutest expression, hoping Abigail would drop a piece of bacon on the floor.

"It smells *wunderbaar*," Jeremiah said, taking a seat at the head of the table.

"Oh good! Cooking bacon is the easiest way to get everyone moving in the morning around here," Abigail chuckled. "I expect to see Jo and Emma come running in here anytime now."

As if on cue, Abigail and Jeremiah's children entered the room, dressed almost identical to their parents.

"Oh, man, I'm starving," Jo said, settling in next to his father.

"Me, too," Emma said, stuffing a handful of colored pencils into her pink backpack that sat on the floor by the dining room table.

"*Vell, gut mariye*," Abigail said to both of them, and they responded the same in unison.

"You were right about the bacon," Jeremiah said to Abigail, chuckling. Then turning his attention to the kids, he said, "I don't think I heard either of you ask if your *maem* needed any help." Emma had just settled in next to Jo.

The children turned and looked at Abigail, politely asking how they could help. Abigail adored the contrast of their light eyes and light skin against their dark hair. The two of them were each a perfect blend of Abigail and Jeremiah, in both their physical looks, as well as their personalities. Emma was outgoing and confident like her mother and artistic like her father. Little Jonah, nicknamed Jo, was quiet and pensive like his father, but smart as a whip and observant like his mother.

"*Nae, denki*. Breakfast is ready," Abigail said, as she set the plate of crispy bacon on the table next to the bowl of breakfast potatoes. "Help yourself," she said. She turned and grabbed the pan of cheesy eggs off the stove next and scooped a healthy portion onto Jeremiah's plate before dividing the rest among Jo, Emma and her own plate. Jeremiah poured coffee into his and Abigail's coffee mugs as Abigail sat down at the table opposite of Jo, on the other side of her husband. Angel settled at Abigail's feet, and Abigail slipped her a pinch of bacon fat under the table.

After a few moments of quiet breakfast prayers, the family chatted in between bites about their upcoming day. Emma talked about the homework she had completed the night before, and Jo shared fun details about the latest book he was reading. After breakfast was finished, the children cleared the table and began to wash their plates, silverware and juice glasses as Jeremiah gathered his things and headed off to work, wishing everyone a good day.

Abigail next collected the children's lunches, stuffing them into each respective backpack. Then, she went through her daily checklist with each of them, as they slipped on their shoes.

"Do you have your homework?" Abigail asked.

"*Jah*," the children responded at the same time.

"Do you have your prayer books?" she asked next.

"*Jah*," the children again responded in unison.

"Did you say goodbye to Angel?" Abigail asked.

Angel walked slowly in front of the children, waiting to be petted goodbye as she was every school morning. The children both rubbed her fur and wished Angel a good day before slipping their arms into their backpacks and heading toward the door.

"Wait a minute," Abigail said to the children. They paused at the door, their eyes cast up at their mother with curiosity. Emma's hand rested on the handle of the front door.

"What about me? Do I get a goodbye hug?" Abigail grinned, her hands on her hips. Smiles spread across the children's faces. Jo was the first to wrap his arms around Abigail's waist and squeeze tight. Emma stood behind her brother, patiently waiting her turn.

"*Gut daag, Maem*," he said, his voice muffled, his face buried in her apron.

"*Denki*, Jo," Abigail said. "Be *gut* today."

Jo turned and headed toward the door, but he waited for his sister before exiting.

"*Gut daag, Maem*," Emma said, hugging her arms lightly around Abigail's neck. "*Denki* for breakfast. It was *wunderbaar*."

"You're getting so tall, Emma," Abigail said. "Slow down growing up, would you?" she teased.

Emma smiled. "No way," she said with a broad mischievous grin. The young girl turned back to Jonah and muttered, "Come on, let's go," as the two of them headed out the door. Angel curled up on the rug in front of the couch and chewed on her bone.

Abigail stood at the door for a few minutes, watching as the two of them met up with their friends on the road in front of their home. She smiled as they headed up the road together, full of energy. The family had moved to the town of Billingsley only months before, and it made her very happy to see how adjusted the children had become in such a short time.

She returned her attention to the kitchen to finish cleaning up after breakfast and then headed back to her room to finish getting herself ready for the day. She looked at the clock and quickly did the math in her head to determine that she had about an hour before she could expect her friend Rose to appear at her doorstep, ready to go. The two ladies were going to drive into town together and do some grocery shopping for the upcoming week.

Abigail filled her teapot halfway with water and set it on the burner, turned on high heat. She flipped through her selection of tea, settling upon one of her morning favorites, a double bergamot. Once her tea was prepared, she headed to the couch to sit and enjoy the peace and quiet. She leaned over and scratched Angel behind the ear before leaning back and curling her feet under her skirt on the comfortable old couch. She picked up her grocery list that she had placed on the table next to her the night before, and looked to see if she had accounted for everything she needed.

Her thoughts were interrupted just a minute later as Angel jumped to her feet and barked loudly at the door.

"What is it, girl?" Abigail asked. She set her tea cup down on the table and looked out the large picture windows of the living room. She watched as her friend Rose hurried up the front lawn. Rose's face was red and she was visibly upset. Abigail glanced back at the clock. There was still plenty of time before they had agreed to meet.

Rose knocked loudly on the front door and called out, "Abigail, it's me!"

Hearing the urgency in her friend's voice, Abigail rushed to the door and swung it open. Without another word, Rose fell into Abigail's arms and pressed her face into her shoulder. Rose's body shook as she wept, and Abigail stood with her quietly, letting her cry before asking her any questions.

Rose lifted her face and wiped her face with a handkerchief she pulled out of her apron pocket. "Rose," Abigail said, squeezing her free hand with her own. Rose's cheeks were tear-stained, her nose and eyes red. "What has happened?" Abigail asked quietly.

Rose wiped her face again and took a deep breath, but tears continued to fall slowly down her cheeks.

"It's *baremlich*, Abigail," Rose said. "I can't believe it." She shook her head, and wiped her nose before continuing. "It's Charlie," she said. Abigail knew instantly that Rose was referring to Rose's younger sister, Charlotte.

Rose looked as if just saying her sister's name might be too much to bear.

"What happened? Is she okay?" Abigail asked, now holding tight to Rose's shoulders as if to help her stand.

Rose shook her head and sobbed, wiping her nose again.

"She's dead, Abigail," Rose said in a voice barely above a whisper. Abigail gasped. She stood, with her mouth slightly open, in complete shock before responding. She couldn't even be sure she'd heard Rose's words correctly. Abigail knew Charlotte to be a young healthy woman in her late-twenties. Charlotte was an inspiration to so many young women, especially the Amish, fully owning her own flower shop at her age and establishing a reputation as a talented floral designer.

"*Ach du lieva*," Abigail finally found her words. "I am so sorry, Rose." She pulled Rose close to her for another hug, fighting tears herself. She wanted to ask what happened, but she knew she needed to wait and let Rose tell her when she was ready to say the words.

After a moment, Rose muttered, "Who could've done this, Abigail? How could *Gotte* let this happen to her?"

Abigail's skin was instantly covered in goosebumps and she felt a sense of familiarity that formed a pit in her stomach.

"What?" Abigail said, again grabbing Rose's shoulders and standing her up, so she could see her face. "Are you saying that your sister was murdered, Rose?" Abigail heard the words escape from her mouth as if her voice echoed in an empty cave.

Rose nodded her head, her eyes filled up with tears again. She fell back into Abigail's arms, sobbing uncontrollably.

Abigail comforted her friend as her mind raced. *How could this be happening?* she thought to herself. She just couldn't believe there had been another murder in Billingsley. It had only been a few months since the last murder in town, and even though the killers had been arrested, the community was still reeling with fear.

And Charlotte? Who in the world would ever want to kill Charlotte?

Chapter Two

A bigail slipped on her shoes and wrapped her shawl around her shoulders. She stood by the front door, tapping her foot, waiting for Jeremiah. Picking up the basket of fresh rolls she had baked for the dinner, she checked to make sure the towel was tucked securely on the edges to keep them warm.

"*Denki* for watching Jo and Emma tonight, Faith," Abigail spoke to the blonde teenager sitting in the middle of the living room, playing cards with the children. "I know it was last minute."

"You're *velcome*," Faith said, her voice kind and soft. "I'm happy to help," she said.

"*Vell*, you're a lifesaver," Abigail said and then cringed slightly at her choice of words before continuing. "We shouldn't be too long. We are only having dinner and will be back before Jo and Emma's bedtime."

Faith nodded and returned her attention to the game.

Emma nudged her babysitter, whispering, "It's your turn," and Faith played an ace of hearts.

"There is a casserole on the counter for the three of you for dinner. Please try to eat around six o'clock to stay on schedule," Abigail continued, looking at the clock. She was starting to wonder what could be taking Jeremiah so long.

"Ready!" Jeremiah called out as he entered the room and rushed to Abigail's side. He grabbed his light jacket off the coat rack.

"Hugs goodbye, please," Abigail said to the kids. Jo and Emma scrambled to their feet just long enough to hug their parents' goodbye before hurrying back to pick up their cards.

Abigail had not told the children yet about Charlotte. All they knew was that there was an adult gathering of some sort, and they had no reason to question otherwise. She wasn't even sure if Faith knew the reason for the dinner, but assumed she must, considering her older teen age.

Jeremiah held the door open for Abigail. She handed him the bread basket to hold as she bent down to rustle the fur on Angel's neck.

"You take care of the kids, too, Angel," she whispered in her ear. "We'll be back soon." Angel blinked slowly but made no effort to stand up and see the couple out the door.

Pulling her shawl tighter around her chest, Abigail retrieved the basket from Jeremiah and stepped out into the cool weather. Jeremiah followed, shutting the door behind him. The sun hung low in the sky, casting an orange glow on the row of houses that lined the street.

"Shall we?" he said, holding his arm out for Abigail before they walked down the porch steps together. The couple walked at a steady pace up the road toward the building used for community gatherings. They remained silent, lost in their own thoughts.

The Baker family was the newest addition to the Amish community in Billingsley, so their house sat at the far end of a straight road, neighbors only on one side, facing west. The homes were built in order from the closest to the highway at the end of the road to the furthest, so it was always easy for Abigail to tell who had lived here the longest.

Abigail and Angel took this walk up the road a few times each day, passing all the other matching houses along the way, waving, and sometimes stopping to chat with anyone in sight. Tonight, the evening felt much more gloomy knowing that one of their beloved community members, Charlotte, was no longer with them.

As they approached the others, Jeremiah excused himself to greet the men and Abigail walked the final few steps into the small building, basket in hand. She could hear the familiar sound of bustle and commotion of dinner tables being set up on the long tables in the center of the room mixed with low levels of conversation among the women inside. As she stepped in, she searched the room for Rose right away. She was seated near the end of the center table with her mother, Gracie Baxter, and a couple other women from the community. She held her mother's hand, leaning in close to her almost in a child-like pose.

Abigail set the basket down on the table with the other side items, greeted some of the ladies with a "*gut daag*," and others with a nod before heading to her friend's side.

Rose lifted her head, looking relieved to see Abigail approaching her. She forced a half smile as Abigail slid onto the chair next to her, placing her hand gently on her shoulder for comfort.

"Hi, Rose," Abigail said. "I'm sorry I didn't get here sooner."

"Oh, it's fine," Rose said, blinking back tears. "I'm glad you're here."

Gracie lifted her head and Abigail greeted her next. "Gracie, I'm so sorry to hear about what happened. May Charlotte rest in peace."

A single tear trickled down Gracie's weathered cheek, and she nodded.

"We are praying for you," Abigail said. "Please let me know if there is anything more I can do for you and your family. I am here for you all."

Gracie reached over and squeezed Abigail's hand. "*Denki*," she said. "You are a good friend to Rose, Abigail. It is good to see you here."

Abigail covered Gracie's hand with her own and nodded. Again, her heart ached for Charlotte's family. She couldn't imagine what it must be like to lose someone you love. Only once, a few years ago, had she attended a funeral of someone who was a victim of a crime. It happened in Little Valley, where she had lived all of her life before moving to Billingsley. The deacon's young daughter was kidnapped and died in custody, and Abigail remembered the same sadness on the faces of those closest to the poor child.

She swallowed hard, pushing back the tears of compassion and empathy she felt surfacing.

Abigail turned to look at the door she had entered earlier to see the men filing in, quiet and straight-faced. Her eyes were immediately drawn to Adam Peachey, Charlotte's husband. His face was pale, and his expression was sullen. She noticed he wasn't wearing a jacket of any kind and his shoulders were rounded, his hand stuffed deep into his pants pockets as if he were cold. She glanced over at Jeremiah who was chatting quietly with Peter Amman near the end of the table where she had placed her bread basket.

"Can I please have everyone's attention?" Bishop Andrew Nisley said in a loud voice. He was an older man, his frame tall and thin with a slight bulge in the middle. His beard was long and full, and mostly all gray, matching the thinning hair that peeked out from below his broad-rimmed hat.

The room's low murmur of chatting grew quiet and Abigail watched as Adam fidgeted, kicking his foot gently on the table leg in front of him. She thought he looked like a lost four-year-old boy that was fighting tears.

"*Denki* for gathering here tonight," the bishop began. "I know that it is devastating news that brings us together, but it is also times like this when we need our community the most."

Abigail watched as Adam glanced toward the door. He looked as if he wanted to flee. Jeb Swarey, Rose's husband, stepped over and gently patted Adam on the back, leaning in and whispering something in his ear. Adam nodded.

Adam looked at least ten years younger than his brother-in-law, Jeb, and Abigail wondered how someone so young would manage losing his wife to such a crime. The two had only been married a few years. There were no children yet, which was unusual, but Abigail remembered Rose telling her once how the young couple were trusting in *Gotte* that it would happen for them in due time.

"We must find gratitude even in the times of loss." The bishop continued, "Let's pray together and thank *Gotte* for this *wunderbaar* food and community."

Everyone in the room bowed their heads and folded their hands in front of them. A few moments of silence embraced them all, providing a stillness that was comforting and peaceful.

"Let's eat," Bishop Nisley said, and the silence was drowned out by the sound of chairs being pushed away from the table, plates and silverware clinking together, and quiet conversation returned.

Abigail met Jeremiah's eyes as he approached her from across the room. "Are you ready to eat, Abby?" he asked.

"*Jah,*" Abigail said before turning to ask Rose and Gracie if they needed anything.

"*Nae, denki,*" Rose said, standing on her feet and looking around the room. "I'm going to find Jeb."

"Oh, he's right over..." Abigail began, nodding toward the door where she last saw Jeb speaking with Adam, but her sentence was interrupted by a loud commotion.

"NO!" Adam yelled, shaking his arm free of Jeb's grip and knocking over a casserole bowl that sat precariously near the edge of the table. Several women gasped, but the rest of the room fell tensely silent.

"I'm not!" He screamed, his beet red face only inches from Jeb's. His words were fierce and full of anger and frustration. He quickly surveyed the room before turning and running out the door. Jeb followed right behind him, calling out his name.

Rose fled past Abigail and Jeremiah, in pursuit of her husband and brother-in-law.

A familiar pit grew inside Abigail's stomach and she instantly felt uneasy.

Something was not right, she could tell.

Chapter Three

Chief Amy Edwards sighed as she shifted her patrol car into park outside of the police station. Charlotte Peachey was the third murder in Billingsley in the last few months, and she was perplexed as to how, and why, this kept happening. Billingsley was such a peaceful town when she had first arrived a few years prior. She expected to serve a town that had a few small crimes here and there, but nothing like murder. And certainly not one murder right after the other.

The main emergency line was forwarded to Amy's cell phone after hours, and she had just headed for bed the night that Brett Holden had called her to tell her that he had found Charlotte lying dead on the floor of her flower shop. She remembered Charlotte as the young pretty Amish girl who was always friendly with a wave from the other side of the glass whenever she would pass the shop. She had engaged in a couple casual conversations with her when visiting the Amish community, as well. Charlotte's shop had quickly become successful soon after it opened. Everyone who had ever ordered or received flowers from Blooms and More knew in an instant just how talented Charlotte was when it came to floral design. She would create the most beautiful bouquets. Gracie Baxter once told Chief Edwards that her youngest daughter, Charlotte, "Could make a bouquet of carnations look expensive."

Chief Edwards opened the door to the police station and hung her backpack purse on the back of her chair before heading to the back of the large open room to brew a pot of coffee. She was the first one there and enjoyed the peace and quiet that greeted her in the early mornings. The sound of the coffee pot bubbling and steaming was the only noise that could be heard as she settled in her worn leather chair, her mind racing to solve the crime of Charlotte's murder.

The long center drawer of her antique mahogany desk creaked as she pulled it open to retrieve a pad of pink sticky notes and a pen. Her desk was covered in stacks of papers that at first glance would seem like a mess, but to the chief, each stack made sense and she was confident that she knew where and what everything was.

She pushed a smaller stack of papers aside to make room for the little square pad of sticky notes. She had found this method of brainstorming to be the most helpful to her in the past, and she thoroughly enjoyed the practice of collecting and disposing of the notes after the case was solved.

Chief Edwards took a deep breath and wrote one name on the first note: Adam. She fidgeted in her chair and set the pen down on the desk, staring at the name in front of her. She didn't want to believe that Adam Peachey had anything to do with his wife's murder, but it didn't take a seasoned investigator to know the first suspect is always the person closest to the victim. She knew she had to rule Adam out before moving on to anyone else, and she hadn't been able to do that yet.

Adam had no alibi for the evening Charlotte was killed. He said he was home alone, but no neighbors, friends or family could confirm that.

He also didn't report her missing when she didn't come home from work on time that evening. Chief Edwards found this suspicious, especially when Adam confirmed that his wife typically closed shop and arrived home by six o'clock to cook dinner.

Her thoughts were interrupted by the aroma of freshly brewed coffee. She set down her pen and returned to the back of the room to pour the steaming liquid into her favorite mug. The mug was shaped like a bear's claw and the caption "Grin and bear it" was printed on one side.

The chime on the door rang and Chief Edwards called out, "Good morning!" while adding a packet of sugar to her coffee and without turning around.

"Chief Edwards?"

The chief of police was surprised to hear a female voice. She expected a fellow police officer, specifically Officer Andrew Stokes who always arrived first after she did. She dropped her spoon on the counter and spun around to find Rose Swarey standing in front of the door.

Rose was wearing a plain country blue dress that fell just a few inches above the floor. A white simple apron with deep pockets laid over the dress, tied around her waist. Rose looked as neat as a new pin with her hair pulled back and tucked under a crisp white *kapp*, but Chief Edwards noticed right away that her eyes looked tired and her face was pale.

"Rose," Chief Edwards said, her voice kind and soft. "I didn't expect to see you here."

"I know," Rose said, wringing her hands in front of her. She reminded the chief of a small girl, nervous and shy.

"Please, have a seat," Chief Edwards said, rushing over to push one of the guest chairs over to sit in front of her desk. "You'll have to excuse the mess," she said, gesturing to the piles of paper on her desk.

Rose thanked her and took a few steps toward the empty chair. The chief watched as Rose's eyes drifted to the sticky note in the center of her desk with Adam's name written on it.

Chief Edwards settled in her chair and slid open the noisy drawer again to pull out a standard yellow pad of paper.

"Are you the only one here?" Rose asked, sounding surprised.

"Yes, I like to get here bright and early before everyone else," the chief responded, "but Officer Stokes should wander in here before too long."

Rose sat quietly, looking at her hands folded in her lap.

"What can I do for you, Rose?" Chief Edwards had planned to visit Rose later that day to ask questions, but this made things easier.

"I'm here to see how I can help find my sister's killer," Rose said, her demeanor changing from quiet to eager. "I know it has only been a little over a day since she was killed, but I read somewhere that if you don't solve the crime in forty-eight hours, your chances of finding the killer become much more difficult."

Chief Edwards took a deep breath and exhaled slowly before answering.

"That is true," she said, nodding, "but we don't have very many clues, I'm afraid."

Rose sat quietly. The chief thought Rose might be blinking away tears, but she couldn't be sure. She leaned in towards the desk and assured Rose with a soothing voice. "I'm confident we'll get to the bottom of it, though, Rose."

Rose nodded, her eyes welling up with tears.

"So, since you're here, why don't you tell me about Charlotte?"

Rose slumped back in her chair and pulled a handkerchief out of her apron pocket, dabbing at her eyes. She looked relieved to be asked about her sister. Her voice cracking, she began to tell Chief Edwards all about Charlotte.

"She was only twenty-five years old, you know," Rose began.

Chief Edwards nodded her head.

"And she was so amazing, Chief. She really was." Rose's words came pouring out of her mouth as if she had been holding a secret for too long.

"She truly was the whole package. She was smart and so ambitious. She impressed all of us in the family when she announced that she was going to open her own flower shop. And then, she entered some floral design contest and actually won first prize. We were all so excited for her. I made her favorite strawberry pie and put extra whipped cream on top, just like she liked, to celebrate her win." Rose stopped and wiped away a new tear that had escaped from her eye.

Chief Edwards smiled politely and then suddenly realized that she hadn't offered Rose anything to drink. "Oh, my gosh, I don't mean to interrupt you, but I just realized I didn't offer you a cup of coffee. Would you like coffee or tea or water?"

Rose shook her head and thanked her.

"Okay, so where were we?" the chief asked. "Yes, her flower shop and her award. Please do go on. Ignore my interruption."

Rose continued. "I guess you know she and Adam had been trying to have children, but Charlie never got pregnant. The whole community prayed for them to start a family. Charlie didn't really like to talk about it, but we all knew that not having children was a big reason behind all the work she put in at the shop."

"And Adam?" the chief interjected, "Was Adam equally disappointed that they weren't able to easily have children?"

"Oh, of course," Rose said without hesitation. "It is our culture to have children right away in a marriage. I know they were both very disappointed, but we hardly ever spoke of it."

Chief Edwards wanted to make a note to follow up about this, but felt it might be rude, so she refrained from doing so.

"I know the two of you were sisters, but would you consider your relationship with Charlotte a close one?" the Chief asked. "What I mean is, did the two of you talk often and trust each other with secrets?"

"I think so," Rose said. "Charlie was a bit younger than me, almost eight years younger, but as we became adults, our bond as sisters became stronger." Rose wiped her eyes.

"That's very nice," the chief responded. Then after a short pause, she asked the most important question. "Do you know anyone who would want to hurt your sister, Rose?"

Rose sat quietly for a moment, her eyes fell on the sticky note on the chief's desk where the name Adam was scribbled and shook her head.

"No, I honestly have no idea who could have…" her words trailed off and tears quickly sped down her face. She turned her face down to her lap and held up her hand as if to apologize, holding the handkerchief over the bridge of her nose between her eyes.

"It's okay, Rose," the chief said, waiting patiently. "I am so sorry for your loss. Charlotte was a special girl. Please let me know if I can get you anything."

Rose shook her head.

"I'm fine," she said. She wiped her eyes one more time and raised her face to meet Chief Edwards' eyes with her own. "One thing I do know is that anyone who knew Charlie would never want to hurt her."

The chief nodded, but she couldn't help but silently wonder if that was true, considering the only evidence she had.

Chapter Four

A ngel began barking at the living room windows, her tail wagging furiously back and forth. Abigail quickly slipped the last of the freshly laundered and folded kitchen towels into the cupboard and glanced around the room for anything out of place. On her way to the front door, she caught a glimpse of her mother, Beth Troyer, stepping out of the Amish taxi in front of her house. She squealed with excitement and threw the door open.

"*Wilkumme, Maem!*" she called out, standing on the doorstep, her arms outstretched.

Beth was grinning from ear to ear as she walked briskly up the porch steps to embrace Abigail in a big bear hug, swaying her side to side.

"My *dochder*!" she said. "It's so *gut* to see you!"

"Oh, you too, *Maem*," Abigail responded, her eyes squeezed tight.

"Here's your luggage, madam," the driver said, placing Beth's simple tapestry bag at the top of the porch steps. "Have a *gut* time, and I'll be back on Sunday to pick you up."

"*Denki*," Beth responded, politely. She was not as outgoing as her daughter, and Abigail made up for it by thanking him again.

Abigail picked up the bag and wrapped her arm around her mother's waist, ushering her inside.

"How was the trip up here?" she asked, sincerely curious.

"It was *gut*," Beth said. "I mostly read a new mystery book that I picked up at the library just for this trip."

Abigail grinned. She figured her mother spent the whole trip reading. Beth began to tell her daughter all about the plot and how she suspected the story would end as Abigail proceeded to fill and turn on the teakettle at the stove, glancing over occasionally to stay engaged in the conversation.

"*Vell*, enough about that," Beth said. "I want to hear how things are going here in Billingsley. The driver mentioned that there was another murder, Abigail. And this time, she was an Amish girl! I was shocked when I heard the news!"

"*Jah*, it's true," Abigail said. "And, *Maem*, Charlotte was Rose's younger sister."

Beth gasped. "No! *Ach du lieva*, that's *baremlich*!" She clasped her hands together and bowed her head, saying a quick silent prayer.

Abigail set the teacups and the honey on the table, dropping Earl Grey tea bags in each. She turned to collect the hot kettle and slowly poured water into the cups, one by one.

"*Denki, dochder*," Beth said, reaching for a cup and playing with the strings of the tea bag, moving the bag up and down methodically. "How are Rose and the rest of her family? Was Charlotte married? Do they know who killed her?"

Abigail sat down across the table from her mother, took a deep breath, and proceeded to fill her in on everything she knew, including what Rose had shared about her visit at the police station. Beth sat quietly, captively listening to each and every detail. Abigail knew her mother well enough to know that her mind must be racing, trying to solve the case.

"*Ach du lieva*," Beth said again, when Abigail had finished. "That is a shame that her grieving husband seems to be the primary suspect."

Abigail nodded. She remembered his short outburst at the dinner and how upset he had looked that evening.

"What even would be his motive, though, I wonder?" Abigail said.

"*Jah*, I was thinking the same thing. There has to be another answer," Beth responded. "And there's clearly more to this story than we know. Someone is hiding something."

Abigail's stomach flip-flopped and she desperately wanted to talk about something else.

"How's Aunt Anna?" Abigail asked, beginning to clear the table.

"She's *gut*," Beth said. "She sends her love."

Beth continued catching Abigail up on all the news from her home town of Little Valley, and Abigail appreciated the distraction. She longed to see her extended family and missed everyone terribly. It was wonderful to hear all about their lives.

Abigail next showed her mother the latest crochet project she was working on, as well as spoke about how her sales at the gift shop had grown in the last month. Then she helped Beth get settled in Emma's room and left her to freshen up before they took Angel on an afternoon walk.

"It's so nice out here," Beth said, as they walked along the street, pausing to allow Angel to stop and smell a tree or plant every few feet.

"Hmmmm... I love the start of the Fall season," Abigail agreed.

"When will Emma and Jo be home?"

"Soon, actually," Abigail said. "Their schedule is very similar to what we had at home in Little Valley."

She added, "They are very excited to see their grandmother."

Beth beamed. "I am excited to see them, too." She linked her arm through Abigail's.

As the two passed by Charlotte and Adam's house, Abigail whispered, "That's where Charlotte lived."

Beth glanced over and said, "Oh, the flowers are so pretty."

Abigail nodded.

"You know, that reminds me," Beth said. "Do you remember Eliza Mayer in Little Valley? You know, she works with Matthew at the Secret Garden."

"I faintly remember her," Abigail said. "I'm not sure I ever really met her."

"*Vell*, you know, she also entered a floral design competition. I remember Matthew talking about it one Sunday night at dinner." Matthew was a family friend of theirs.

Abigail had known Matthew from childhood. He was a very kind man, never married. Beth considered him as a son, inviting him to weekly dinners.

"Interesting," Abigail said, mindlessly.

"*Jah*, I remember Matthew saying she was pretty upset when she didn't win," Beth continued. "I guess she had really high hopes of taking the trophy."

"Must have been some competition," Abigail said, gently tugging at Angel's leash to urge her to continue walking.

Beth stopped in her tracks. "And you know what, *dochder*?" she said, her voice lowered and her hand covering her heart.

Abigail felt a sense of dread. She knew she had to ask the followup question, but she wasn't sure if she wanted to hear the answer.

"Goodness sakes, *Maem*, what is it?"

"I just remembered Matthew saying last weekend how busy the shop was because Eliza was out of town," Beth answered, her eyes wide.

"Okay..." Abigail said slowly. She didn't understand what Beth was trying to tell her.

Beth leaned in closer to Abigail. Angel sat at their feet and looked up as if she were also interested in what Beth was about to say.

"And I specifically remember him saying that Eliza was in Billingsley," Beth whispered.

It was Abigail's turn to gasp. Her stomach turned flip flops.

"*Maem*, if you just solved the crime of Charlotte's murder, I'm going to be really impressed."

Chapter Five

The front door of Charlotte and Adam's house flung open and Rose stood on the threshold, calling Abigail's name and waving to get her attention.

"Abigail! Mrs. Troyer! I'm so glad to have caught you!" Rose's nose was red and her cheeks were flushed.

Abigail and Beth walked over to the gate of the small white picket fence that lined the front yard of the Peachey home.

"Hi, Rose!" Abigail responded, and Beth waved. "How are you?"

Rose didn't answer the question. Instead, she waved the ladies inside. "Come in, come in," she insisted, holding the door open and stepping to the left side on the porch.

Abigail and her mother glanced at each other as if to ask if the other had any reservations. Neither spoke, and Abigail unlatched the gate, motioning for her mother to walk ahead of her. Angel followed behind them.

"Mrs. Troyer, I had forgotten you were visiting. It's good to see you," Rose said, as Beth walked up the steps to the front porch.

"*Denki*, Rose," Beth responded. "I am so sorry for your loss. I truly am." Rose nodded in thanks. She hugged Rose lightly before stepping aside to allow for Abigail to greet Rose, as well.

"How are you, Rose?" Abigail asked again, also reaching out with a hug.

"I'm doing okay," Rose said. "I'm here alone going through my sister's things, and I saw the two of you walking by. I thought I would stop you and offer you a cup of tea. I would love the company."

Before Abigail could respond, Beth spoke. "We would love that, *denki*, Rose." And the three of them headed inside, leaving Angel settled in for a nap in the sun on the front porch.

Abigail thought it felt a little strange to be inside Charlotte's house. She had never visited before Charlotte's murder, and it felt almost like an intrusion of some sort.

She wanted to be respectful and tried hard not to look around at her things too much.

"Where is Adam today?" Abigail asked Rose.

Rose shrugged. "Who knows," she said. "He keeps pulling a disappearing act. He and I were supposed to go through Charlie's things today, but when I got here, he was nowhere to be found."

Rose took an already hot kettle off the stove and poured three steaming cups of lavender tea, placing each cup on the small round kitchen table. "Please, have a seat," she said, gesturing toward the rounded back wooden chairs with colorful cushions.

"What a nice home," Beth said, pulling out a seat. "Thank you for inviting us."

"*Jah*, it was... I mean, is... a nice place," Rose stammered. "I always thought it was very cozy and comfortable here."

Abigail nodded and settled in the chair between the other two ladies.

"*Denki* for the tea," Abigail said to Rose. "Is there anything we can do to help you?" Abigail offered, but she secretly hoped Rose would decline. She wasn't sure how she would feel going through Charlotte's things, and she knew Jo and Emma would be home in the next couple hours.

Rose sat quietly for a moment, sipping her tea, as if her mind had escaped to somewhere else. Abigail glanced at Beth again, but Beth was watching the host carefully. She leaned forward and touched Rose's hand. Rose jumped in her seat, startled.

"*Ach du lieva*," Rose said, "I'm sorry. I haven't been sleeping well, and this is... a lot."

Abigail instantly felt remorse for her thoughts of hoping Rose would say she didn't need her help. Clearly, she could use a hand with this daunting task.

"No apologies necessary," Abigail said. "We can help. I'm glad we were walking by today."

"*Jah*, what can we do?" Beth asked sincerely.

Rose took a deep breath and exhaled slowly. "Can you help me pack her things away? I'm not sure if it's too early to do so. I haven't lost anyone before," Rose continued, her words choked. "But, Adam asked for my help. He is really having a hard time with all of this and I want to support him in any way I can. Seeing her things lying around is very upsetting for him."

Beth nodded. "We can certainly help with that. Between the three of us, we should have things packed up in no time."

"*Denki*," Rose said, setting her cup of tea down and pushing her chair. Her eyes looked empty and glazed over, and Abigail wondered how she was able to continue on with the heartache of losing someone so close and dear to her heart. She hoped Rose would be able to find time to heal soon.

Rose led the way to the bedroom with Beth and then Abigail in tow. Walking into the small bedroom, Abigail first saw clothes strewn out on the bed, and a couple boxes folded, lying on the floor. Beth began to fold the dresses carefully. Abigail jumped in to help and Rose stood at the foot of the bed, watching helplessly. She looked as if she were about to burst into tears without a moment's notice.

Abigail walked over and gave her friend another warm hug.

"It's going to be okay, Rose," she said, rubbing her back. She wanted to tell her about Eliza Mayer, but she also didn't want to get her friend's hopes up in finding the killer if it was a dead end. And it just didn't seem like the right time to discuss it.

"What is this?" Beth said, as she bent to pick a piece of folded paper off the floor. She handed it to Rose. "It fell out of one of the dress's pockets," she explained.

Rose carefully and slowly unfolded the paper and began reading out loud.

Dearest Charlie, she began. *I am still working through what you told me that terrible evening. My heart is broken.*

I can't sleep. I can't eat. Your love for someone else is all I think about...

Rose gasped. She looked at Abigail, her mouth open.

"It's signed by Adam," Rose said quietly.

Abigail's eyes were wide. She grasped Rose's arm to steady her. She couldn't believe what she had heard. The room went silent and no one moved for a moment.

"There must be ...some explanation for this... I mean, surely..." Beth stuttered. Abigail watched as her mother tried to find comforting words. Rose stood there, still stunned, the paper rustling in her trembling hand.

"Rose," Abigail whispered. "I'm so sorry."

Rose closed her mouth and carefully refolded the paper, slipping it into her apron pocket without a word.

"We should probably stop here," Beth said. "I think the police might want to search the home."

Abigail watched as a tear slid down Rose's cheek. She reached into her apron pocket and pulled out a handkerchief, handing it to Rose.

Rose nodded at Beth, and wiped her face with the back of her hand. She muttered, "*Denki*, Mrs. Troyer, but I think for now, I'd like to keep this quiet." Her eyes pleaded for understanding as she looked back and forth between Abigail and Beth for agreement.

Chapter Six

Rose sat at the small round table in the seat where Charlotte always sat when they would have tea together. She faced the back door, waiting for Adam to return. Her house was located right next door to Charlotte and Adam's house, so she had returned home to check in on the kids and to prepare a dinner for her family, while keeping one eye out for Adam.

Adam had requested help sorting through Charlotte's things, but he left the house just after Rose had arrived. She certainly wondered if it was a bit premature to pack Charlotte's things, but she wanted to support Adam in any way she could. When she walked in that morning carrying two boxes, Adam was overly emotional, unable to stop the tears from flowing, and he left in a hurry mumbling something about needing a walk to sort his thoughts.

Several hours had passed, and Rose was beginning to get worried. She held the note that Abigail's mother had found earlier that day, turning it over and over slowly in her hands. She thought of how her little sister, Charlie, must have held the paper the same way just days prior to her murder, since it was still tucked away in a dress.

Rose's heart ached that her sister was experiencing some sort of turmoil in those last few days. She could only naturally wonder if it was a clue to why her life was taken. Rose knew she needed to tell the police about the note, but she wanted to confront Adam first and give him a chance to explain some things. As the clock ticked and Adam was nowhere to be found, Rose found herself becoming more and more uncomfortable about the confrontation.

Charlie, tell me what happened, Rose thought to herself. *Who did this to you?*

No matter what the note said, Rose refused to believe that there was infidelity on her sister's part. She couldn't imagine her sister would ever do such a thing. It was not only a sin, but it was a character flaw that just wasn't consistent with who she knew Charlie to be. Rose had no doubt there was either an explanation or a misunderstanding of some kind.

Dusk was starting to settle in, and Rose stood to her feet to gather her things and head home. She was going to tell her husband, Jeb, everything and leave it up to him to decide what to do next with the note and with Adam's disappearance.

She had one hand on the doorknob of the front door when footsteps could be heard on the steps of the back porch. Rose braced herself and felt fearful for the first time in Charlotte's house. She fought the urge to just leave, running for the safe feeling of her own home, husband and family, and instead turned, watching the doorknob of the back door turn and then push open.

Adam entered and hung his hat and light jacket on the coat rack before he noticed Rose was standing by the front door.

"*Ach du lieva*," he cried out. "You startled me!"

Rose felt an odd sense of satisfaction with that and realized her worry about his absence had turned into anger.

"*Gut*," she snapped. "Where have you been? I've been worried sick and was about to send Jeb out to find you."

Adam waved his hand in the air as if to disregard her question. "I'm fine," he said. Rose realized his voice sounded huskier than normal as if he were fighting a cold but figured it was probably due to crying spells instead.

Adam went to the cupboard and pulled out a loaf of bread and a jar of peanut butter and began to make himself a sandwich, ignoring Rose completely.

Rose took a deep breath. As irritated as she was, she had no desire to nag her sister's husband, and she wanted to be sensitive to his grief and heartache. She walked towards the table and sat back down in the seat she had occupied before, when she was waiting for Adam. She noticed the cushion was still warm.

Adam turned with his sandwich in hand and leaned against the counter, taking a big bite.

Rose noticed his fingernails were dirty and his face tear-stained with what must be sweat and dirt, as well. She knew Adam felt at peace in the woods and she could only assume that is where he had disappeared for the day, to find comfort.

"Adam," Rose said, making an effort to keep her voice even-keeled. "I found a note that you wrote Charlie in one of her dress pockets."

Adam froze. He stopped chewing and his eyes grew wider.

"Okay," he said quietly. His hand dropped by his side, barely still hanging on to the remaining half of his sandwich.

Rose nodded. "*Jah*, it's okay, Adam. I haven't shown the note to anyone," she said, cringing a little knowing that it wasn't the full truth. It's true that she hadn't shown the note to anyone, but she also didn't say that Abigail and Mrs. Troyer were present when the note was found.

Adam walked toward the table and sat down across from Rose, setting his sandwich directly on the wood without a plate or a napkin.

"So, the secret is out," Adam said. He took another bite but didn't attempt to elaborate at all.

"Remember, Adam, the truth doesn't have to be liked. It only has to be spoken. The truth may hurt, but it will set you free." Rose said, inviting Adam to share his burdens.

Adam let out a long sigh and ran his hands through his thick hair.

"My wife was having feelings for another man," he said, his voice thick and heavy.

Rose stifled a gasp and shook her head slightly. "That's hard to believe, Adam," she said matter-of-factly.

Adam burst into a sort of maniacal laughter, and it shook Rose to the core. She braced herself by instinctively holding on tightly to the table.

"That's what I said!" Adam said loudly. "I thought Charlie was playing some kind of weird joke on me when she first confessed."

Rose sat very still and waited for Adam to continue.

"And then when I realized she was serious, I thought that *Gotte* must be punishing me for something," he continued, his words poured out and fresh tears fell down his face. "I couldn't talk to her. I couldn't even look at her without feeling something terrible. I was angry. I was sad. I was jealous." His eyes narrowed as he spit out the last word.

"I'm so sorry..." Rose began, but Adam wasn't finished and he interrupted her.

"I haven't slept well one night since she told me," he said, wiping his face with the back of his hand. "I was filled with confusion. I never expected anything like this. Who does, right?" he chuckled again, dropping his hand hard on the table.

Rose pulled away slightly and considered leaving abruptly, but she wanted to know more. She sat silent as Adam continued.

Adam fell forward, holding his head in his hands, his elbows perched on the table. He started to cry, openly sobbing. "I was mostly filled with shame, you know?" he said, his words jumbled. "And heartache. I've never felt such pain before."

"*Jah*, I know it must've been *baremlich*," Rose said, fighting her own tears.

"I couldn't talk to her about it. Heck, I couldn't talk to anyone about it for that matter. So, I wrote letters and gave them to her," Adam continued. "I wanted to save my marriage, but I wasn't ready to forgive her yet. And I was scared what it would mean if the bishop found out. I didn't want her to be shunned. I was sure that would just drive her into the other man's arms."

Rose took a deep breath. This was definitely a messy situation, and she was struggling so hard to comprehend that her little sister would actually fall for someone else when she was married. Everything Adam was saying was overwhelming.

"Who was it?" Rose asked, timidly.

Adam lifted his head and looked Rose directly in the eyes. "I don't know. I honestly don't know," he answered, before resting his head in his hands again. "I didn't want to know anything more."

"So, she didn't tell you anything else?" Rose asked, daring to push a bit further.

Adam cried into his hands, sobbing, before responding. "She said..." he hesitated, and Rose leaned forward. "She said he was a customer at the shop."

Rose's mind raced a million miles an hour. Adam didn't say it but she knew what he meant. Charlotte was having feelings for an *Englischer*. She wasn't sure if that made things worse, but it certainly didn't make things better.

Chapter Seven

Rose knocked softly on Abigail's door. Angel's barks drowned out voices from behind the door. Abigail opened the door and met Rose with a surprised expression.

"Oh, hi, Rose!" Abigail said. "Is everything okay? We just finished dinner. Come on in!" Abigail opened the door wide as an invitation.

Rose could see Mrs. Troyer sitting at the table with the kids, setting up a board game, and Jeremiah settled in the easy chair, petting Angel who had settled on the floor in front of him. She immediately regretted the timing of her visit and wondered if she should just excuse herself, apologize and head home. She wasn't even sure why she had come over to Abigail's house before running home to her husband, Jeb, but something drew her here instead.

Abigail must've picked up on Rose's hesitation because she grabbed her shawl off the coat rack next to the door and said, "Actually, I was just about to take Angel for a walk. Would you like to join me?"

Rose let out a sigh of relief and nodded. "I'll wait here while you get Angel ready," she said, motioning toward the porch swing, and Abigail agreed. Just less than a minute later, Abigail and Angel were outside, ready to go. Rose followed them down the porch steps and out into the street.

"*Denki*, Abigail," Rose started. "I hate to pull you away from your mother's visit and your family time in the evening like this, but I really need to talk to you."

Abigail waved her hand in the air and said, "Of course, Rose. No worries. *Maem* is spending time with the kids and I needed to take this ol' girl out for a walk anyway."

The two friends headed up the street with Angel walking lazily beside them.

"Abigail, I talked to Adam. He was gone all afternoon, but when he came back, he told me everything," Rose blurted out in a loud whisper, looking around to make sure no one was listening.

Abigail moved in closer, walking side by side next to her friend, bringing comfort in her silence as she listened to Rose recount the conversation.

"*Ach du lieva*," Abigail said when Rose finished. "First of all, I'm so sorry, Rose. It sounds like you were very brave approaching Adam."

Rose wiped away a tear.

"And I know it's *baremlich* to hear his truth," Abigail said. "It is very shocking, but please try to remember, we still only have one side of the story. It is devastating what happened to Charlotte, and we also don't have her here to tell us her truth."

Rose nodded, and confessed that she never doubted Adam's account of the story even though the whole thing seemed so far out of her sister's character.

"Regardless, you must take the note, and everything you just told me, to Chief Edwards. She will want to search the house and may find more clues leading to solving the case and putting Charlotte's killer in jail," Abigail continued.

"I know you're right," Rose said, nodding again. Her stomach was upset thinking about how quickly the word will get out to everyone about this, whether it was true or not. Billingsley was a small town, and word traveled fast. Especially a juicy, ugly rumor like this one. She understood why Adam didn't want anyone to know. If it were true, it would not only be embarrassing directly for him, but it could tarnish the whole community's reputation.

"You could ask Chief Edwards to keep it under wraps until she finds out more," Abigail said, as if she were reading Rose's mind. "I bet she would accommodate that."

Rose nodded again, reaching into her pocket to find her handkerchief and blowing her nose.

"And who knows," Abigail said. "Maybe it will turn out to be nothing."

Rose stopped and touched Abigail's arm to do the same. She asked the question that had been gnawing at her mind, but was terrifying to say out loud. "Do you think Adam killed Charlie, Abigail?"

Abigail emphatically shook her head. "No," she responded without hesitation. "No, I do not."

Rose released the breath she was holding and started to cry. Abigail reached out and pulled her to her shoulder, gently rubbing her back.

"It's going to be okay, Rose," Abigail said in a soft voice. "I know this has to be so hard. You've had an incredibly difficult past couple of days, and I just want you to know how impressed I am with you being able to keep it together for everyone. Your sister would be proud of you."

Rose continued to sob, her face hidden in Abigail's shoulder. It was the first time since she had first heard the terrible news that she was able to really express her emotions, and she was so grateful for the opportunity to do so. After the tears slowed down, she lifted her head and wiped her face with the handkerchief, blowing her nose again.

"*Denki*, Abigail," she said softly. "You are a true friend."

"Anytime you need me," Abigail said, "I'll be here, Rose. Anything you need..."

Rose took a deep breath and felt a bit stronger. She was relieved to hear that Abigail did not think Adam was guilty. She trusted her friend's instincts more than her own right now.

The ladies continued their walk up the road, toward Rose's home.

"I will go to the police station again in the morning," Rose said. "And I think I should probably go and make sure things are in order at the shop, as well. Chief Edwards mentioned they have finished their search and investigation there. Adam seems to be quite the mess, so I know that Charlie would want me to be in charge of making decisions about what happens next with the shop."

Abigail nodded. "*Maem* and I do not have plans tomorrow. We would be happy to assist you with anything you need help with there. You know, she's quite the business woman."

"That would be *wunderbaar*," Rose said. "I would really appreciate that. I haven't been there since..." Her words trailed off, and the sick feeling returned to her stomach. She had been dreading seeing where her sweet sister's life was taken from her and she wasn't sure how that would go.

They approached Rose's home and stood for a minute together at the edge of her yard.

"Let's plan it then," Abigail said, distracting Rose from her thoughts. "What time do you want to go? We'd be happy to join you at the police station, as well, since it's on the way. And we should have lunch at Gladness and Joy. We haven't been there in a while."

Rose smiled. Gladness and Joy was their favorite restaurant in town and the two friends had eaten there often. It was a place of good memories and something she could look forward to. "*Jah*, all of that sounds perfect," Rose said. "I will pick you two up at eight o'clock unless that's too early?"

"*Nae*, that sounds *gut*," Abigail said, reaching in for one last hug before saying good night. "Get some rest, friend," Abigail said. "Tomorrow will be tough, but we'll tackle things together one by one."

Rose was filled with a sense of dread, mixed with relief and exhaustion. She looked up at her home, light streaming from the front window. Next door at Charlotte's house, there was no light.

The two friends parted ways, and Rose mounted the porch steps slowly. She stopped and took another deep breath before opening the front door. Tomorrow would be another day, but right now, she needed to sleep.

Chapter Eight

A bigail and her mother, Beth, were ready and waiting on the porch when Rose arrived the next morning in her horse and buggy to pick them up and drive to the police station.

"*Gut mariye*," Rose called out as she pulled to a stop.

Abigail and her mother responded the same in unison as they climbed into the buggy.

"How are you feeling today, Rose?" Abigail asked, reaching over to squeeze her arm affectionately.

"I'm feeling better today. *Denki*. I had a good night's sleep." Rose responded and Abigail did indeed think she had a bit more color in her cheeks than the night before.

"*Gut!*" Abigail exclaimed. "I'm sure you needed that."

"*Denki* for going with me today," Rose said to both Abigail and Beth. "I know it's your vacation and you probably had other plans, Mrs. Troyer.

"Don't be silly," Beth said kindly. "I would rather help a good friend like you than traipse around Billingsley sight-seeing."

"*Jah*, and I think you've already seen all there is to see of Billingsley, *Maem*," Abigail chuckled.

"*Vell*, I am grateful for you," Rose said before flicking the reins to signal the horse to trot up Burnt Mill Road towards the highway.

The three of them chatted about new recipes, fall flowers and late blooming trees, and their kids' latest activities until they arrived in front of the police station. There was no mention of the previous days' events, and Abigail sensed that Rose was also grateful for that.

Entering the police station, Abigail recognized a few of the police officers from interactions during the murder investigation that happened back in the Spring. They exchanged hellos and polite nods. She was starting to think that Chief Edwards was not in the office, when she entered from the back of the room.

"Hello, Good morning!" Chief Edwards called out to them when she saw the three ladies standing near the front door. "Come in, come in!" And then noticing Beth, she greeted her specifically, "Mrs. Troyer, welcome back to Billingsley! It has been a while since we've seen you."

Beth and the chief engaged in small talk for a few minutes and Abigail turned to Rose to check in on her. She appeared pretty calm and collected.

"How are you doing?" she whispered to her friend.

"I'm fine," Rose said. "I guess I'm a little nervous about this whole thing. It's going to get around, you know," she said, referring to the alleged impure thoughts that Charlotte was having about an *Englischer* before her death.

Abigail nodded, "*Jah*, but it could also be a clue that leads to the killer."

"What are you two whispering about over there?" the chief interjected light-heartedly, pulling another chair over to the desk.

Abigail smiled politely.

"I have something I need to tell you, Chief," Rose began. She pulled the note out from her apron pocket and handed it the chief. Then, she proceeded to tell her where she found it and recounted the entire conversation she had with Adam.

Chief Edwards sat and listened attentively without interruption, taking notes.

"Hmmm.." the chief said, looking at the note and leaning back in her seat. "That's quite interesting," she mumbled before returning her focus to Rose. "Thank you for bringing this to me," she said. "I can imagine you want this to remain quiet as long as possible?" She asked the rhetorical question.

"Well, yes," Rose responded. "I was hoping you could keep it confidential as long as you possibly can."

"We don't believe Adam is the one you're looking for, Chief Edwards," Abigail said brazenly. "That's not why we're here."

Rose shot Abigail a grateful look. "That is correct. We want you to dive into a thorough investigation so that you can rule out Adam and find the real culprit as soon as possible."

Chief Edwards nodded. "Well, of course. And this may be very helpful, so thank you again for sharing it with me. I'll need to hold onto it for the investigation."

Rose nodded, "I don't have any reason to want it myself, and I'm pretty sure Adam doesn't want it either. We have a proverb that says, *a happy memory never wears out*, but I think we probably would all want this one to go away."

The chief nodded again, in agreement. "I will take care of it, Rose, I promise. Please let me know if anything else surfaces. Any of you."

Rose, Abigail and Beth agreed and all stood to leave. As they got to the door, Beth turned back around and asked Chief Edwards one final question.

"Oh, Chief Edwards. One more thing. Do you happen to know someone named Eliza Mayer? I think she was traveling here last week. She's a florist, like Charlotte." Beth stood, one hand on the doorknob.

Chief Edwards thought for a few moments before shaking her head. "No, I don't think I do know anyone by that name. Is there any reason to be suspicious about this person? I can ask around," she offered.

Beth shrugged. "Probably not. It may just be a weird coincidence."

Abigail grinned at her mother and then led her outside, after saying polite goodbyes to everyone.

"I guess it was a dead end," she told her mother when they stepped out the door.

"*Jah*, I guess it might have been. Dead ends are good too, though, where there's a mystery. You always want to be able to rule out the innocent suspects." Beth said.

"*Vell*, let's hope Adam is ruled out soon, too, then," Rose said as they climbed into her buggy.

Chapter Nine

R ose pulled her buggy up to the front of the Blooms and More flower shop. It instantly made her sad to see the lights turned off inside and the front stoop empty of fresh potted flowers.

The three women sat in the buggy for a moment before stepping down. The light conversation they were engaging in on the way over from the police station came to a halt.

"Are you okay?" Abigail asked Rose. She reached over and touched Rose's arm. She knew this visit would be exceptionally difficult for her friend.

Rose nodded and took a deep breath. "Let's get this over with," she said. Abigail knew she was referring to the first time here since Charlotte was found shot to death inside those four walls.

"We're here for you, Rose," Beth confirmed. "If you decide once we get in there that you want to leave, we can do that. If you need us to do anything, we're here to help."

Rose looked over at Abigail and Beth, her eyes silently showing gratitude.

"Let's go," she said, pulling the key to the shop out of her purse.

The three women approached the front stoop when the door to the adjoining cigar shop flung open. A strong unpleasant odor of cigar smoke drifted out as if it were a captive cloud trying to escape back into the sky. A large burly man stepped out onto his front stoop and looked Abigail, Rose and Beth up and down.

"Who are you?" his voice boomed.

Beth moved to be the furthest away from him, but Abigail stood taller in her spot.

"Who are you?" she shot the question back his way.

"I'm Fred Goldy. I own this shop," he said, his voice gruff and scratchy.

Rose stepped forward. "Mr. Goldy, I'm Charlotte Peachey's sister. My name is Rose Swarey. We've met before."

Mr. Goldy looked at her, unpleased. He tilted his head, pushing his nose toward the sky.

"Well, no one has been here looking for flowers since your sister was killed there," he said rudely.

"Okay," Abigail interjected. Her brow furrowed. "No one asked you. We'd like to be left alone, please." She emphasized the word please although she had no intention of it sounding kind.

Mr. Goldy huffed, "I'm the one that found her lying there, shot to death."

"We know," Abigail said, unclear as to why he would even mention that to her grieving sister. "There's nothing we need to know about that. Good day, Mr. Goldy."

He stared at Abigail for a long minute and then finally turned and retreated into his shop.

"Whew!" Rose said. "That guy is something else. I don't know how Charlotte ever dealt with him."

"She's a better woman than me, for sure. I would dread having to see him every day," Abigail said, as Rose unlocked the door and pushed it open. She entered, reaching in and turning on the overhead lights.

The first thing the women saw when the shop was illuminated was the outline of Charlotte's body traced on the tile floor - and what appeared to be her blood, now dried, as well. Abigail and Rose stood in shock, but Beth jumped right into action.

"*Vell*, we've got some cleaning to do," she said. "I'll take care of this. You two water the plants."

Abigail appreciated her mother more than ever right then, as she led Rose by the elbow past the outline and behind the counter. Beth headed toward the back storage room and appeared seconds later with a mop and a mop bucket. She headed toward the bathroom to fill the bucket.

Rose stood, wide-eyed, with a blank expression. Abigail guided her to a stool and poured her a paper cup of water from the water cooler at the end of the counter. She placed it in her hand and said, "Take a drink, Rose. It's okay."

Rose robotically lifted the cup to her lips and took a sip, still staring into space. Abigail stood by her, talking to her about the things that needed to be done in hopes that would serve as a distraction while Beth mopped up the remains of the evidence. Every few minutes, Abigail would assure Rose that everything was going to be okay, and eventually, Rose started to recover and respond to questions and comments.

"I'm so sorry, Abigail," Rose said. "I guess I didn't think about how hard this was actually going to be."

"I know," Abigail said, "but please don't apologize. We want to help you." She was so relieved her mother was here to help, too.

Rose looked around at all the flowers, some wilting after a few days of no care, and started crying. "I just can't believe she's gone," she said, her voice cracking.

"I know," Abigail said, rubbing her back. "I know. It's *baremlich*."

"I already miss her so much," Rose said, looking at Abigail with the saddest eyes she had ever seen. Abigail swallowed back her emotions and nodded.

Beth had finished the cleaning and stowed the mop and bucket back in the closet. She came around to the other two girls and hugged Rose, like only a mother could. Rubbing the back of her head, she comforted her as Rose cried in her arms. "It's so hard, honey. I know it is. Your sister was a *wunderbaar* person, but you must trust that this is *Gotte's* will."

Abigail wiped away a stray tear that had escaped from her eye, and wrapped her arms around the two women, squeezing them tightly. The three of them stayed in that pose for a few quiet minutes.

When Rose sat up straight, she thanked them again for being there and excused herself to the bathroom.

"*Maem*," Abigail said. "I'm so glad you're here. I believe *Gotte* sent you to visit just at the right time."

Beth smiled at her daughter. "I'm glad I can help. Rose is strong, but her heart needs to heal, and only *Gotte* can help with that, I'm afraid."

"That's true, but it would certainly speed things up if we knew who did this to Charlotte. It's unbelievable, really, that the life of such a young promising girl was taken so abruptly."

Beth nodded in agreement. "I wonder if there are any uncovered clues in here," she said, looking around.

"I can't imagine there are," Abigail said. "The police did a thorough search, Chief Edwards told us."

Rose exited the bathroom looking much better than when she went in, and she was focused and ready to work.

"Let's throw out the dead flowers," she said. "And let's water the ones that are still alive."

Beth and Abigail jumped into action, following orders, as Rose began looking through the papers in the drawers under the counter.

"I've decided to keep the store open," Rose said, her hands on her hips. "For Charlie."

Abigail smiled warmly. "I think that's a great idea, Rose," she said, but secretly, she wondered how much Rose knew about running a flower shop. Abigail could admit she knew nothing at all about it herself.

"*Vell*, then I think the first step is to make sure you have an accurate inventory," Beth chimed in. "And then, we can find a record of the recent orders and see what we need in stock."

Rose said, "*Jah*, that's a great idea. She pulled out a spiral bound book labeled Inventory on the front cover. Inside were handwritten inventory sheets with weekly dates and added the current date in the top of the left most empty column. Where should we start?"

Beth walked around with Rose and helped her take inventory of everything in the store as Abigail walked around, tidying up and watering what was dry as a bone. After a couple hours of work, Abigail suggested they take a break and grab a bite for lunch. Rose and Beth agreed.

"Next time, you could contact the vendors and place orders based on the inventory numbers she keeps here," Beth said, pointing out the column on the far right. Then, pausing, she said, "Hmmm... that's strange..."

"What is it?" Rose asked and Abigail leaned in for a look, as well.

"*Vell*, it just looks like your sister ordered a lot more gardenias than anything else," Beth said, then looking further, she elaborated. "That's unusual for a flower shop. That's a sort of specialty flower, more expensive than most, and usually a special order kind of thing... but looking here, at the past weeks of inventory, Blooms and More actually sells gardenias every week. She set the book down. It's just strange, is all. Someone around here really likes gardenias, I guess." She shrugged.

"Enough talk about flowers and inventory. Let's go eat. My stomach is growling," Abigail said, and Rose agreed. The three of them collected their things and headed out the door, locking up behind them.

Chapter Ten

The chime on the door of the Gladness and Joy restaurant rang as Abigail, Rose and Beth walked in, alerting the staff at the counter of their arrival.

"*Vilkumme* back to Gladness and Joy!" Sue Renmo called out to them from behind the cash register, with a friendly wave.

Abigail and Rose considered Sue their close friend. She lived a few houses down from Rose and the three of them often gravitated toward each other for company at receptions and other community events. Beth had also visited the restaurant during previous visits and had met Sue prior, as well.

Abigail chose their favorite booth by the front window, and glancing outside, instantly wished she had brought

Angel. Gladness and Joy had free dog treats on the counter, and always kept a fresh bowl of water outside for their customers' pups. Angel had visited the restaurant and sat outside waiting on Abigail on several occasions. It felt almost strange to be here without her.

A young Amish girl dressed in a plain dress with an apron, her hair tied back and tucked into a *kapp*, came over to their table with menus.

"Hi," she said. "Sue told me to tell you to order what you want. It will be on the house, she said."

"Aw, *denki*!" Rose said, "But she doesn't have to do that."

The girl grinned and said, "She said you'd say that, and to just tell you that she wants to." She chuckled. "I'll be back with your waters and to take your order in just a few minutes."

The ladies thanked her again and began discussing the menu. When the young girl returned, they placed their order and then settled in to chat.

"I feel so loved," Rose said, smiling at Abigail and Beth, sitting across the booth from her. "I can't thank you both enough for coming with me today. I really appreciate your help."

"We're so happy to be able to help," Beth said.

"It's no problem at all," Abigail assured her friend.

"Speaking of help, though," Beth said. "What do you need for the funeral tomorrow?"

Rose sighed and slumped back in her chair. "I am so dreading that, but honestly, my mother and her friends are organizing all of it, thankfully. I haven't had to do much but help plan a few small details."

"Oh, that's *wunderbaar*," said Abigail before turning to Beth. "We should check in with Gracie this afternoon and see if we can help with anything."

Beth agreed.

"But, I will say," Rose began, "I would love your help with getting the Blooms and More back open." She looked at Abigail.

"Ah," Abigail said, taking a quick breath. "Rose, I honestly don't know very much about running a flower shop. I don't know the first thing about floral design let alone just the operations of running a business like that."

"I know," Rose said, looking and sounding defeated. "I don't really know much about it either," she paused, "but I think we could learn."

"I definitely want to help you, Rose, you know that, but who is going to teach us how to run the shop?" Abigail continued, after glancing over at her mother who sat quietly next to her. "And, of course, I would have to run it by Jeremiah. I'm responsible for the kids and for putting dinner on the table every night. I just don't know if I'm the right one for this."

"I know. I have thought about all of that. I mean, I have the same responsibilities, but..." Rose pleaded with Abigail, "that shop was Charlie's dream. She put so much work into it. The least I could do is try to keep it open."

Abigail again glanced at her mother. She was curious what she was thinking, but she sat quietly, a bit out of character for her. "*Vell*, I can commit to helping out the first few weeks anyway while the kids are in school, and as long as I am home in time to cook dinner. I mean, we can just let customers know that we aren't prepared to do any special designs or anything, I guess."

Rose let out a small squeak and reached out and grabbed Abigail's hands, squeezing them tight. "Oh, *denki, denki,* Abigail! I will take whatever I can get!"

Abigail smiled back at her friend. She honestly wondered how much help she could be, but she would give it her best shot, just like anything else she committed to doing.

"Okay, we'll start the day after tomorrow. After the funeral," Rose said.

Abigail nodded. "That's fine. *Maem* is leaving that morning, as well, so that will be fine." Then, thinking some more, she teased her mother, "I wonder if Eliza Mayer would be willing to come help." She winked at Beth and Beth rolled her eyes.

"I'm telling you, I thought I heard she was visiting up here last weekend!" Beth insisted. "I think Anna is right;I read too many mysteries." The women laughed together.

Abigail found herself present in the moment and realized that the mood had shifted rather positively just in the last couple hours, and she said a quiet prayer of gratitude for healing as their delicious food was served.

Chapter Eleven

S ue, the owner of Gladness and Joy, stopped by their
table just as the ladies were taking their last bites.
She threw her arm around Rose's shoulders and squeezed
tight.

"I'm thinkin' about you," she said. "Let me know if
there's anything I can do."

"*Denki*, Sue," Rose said.

"I've already talked to your *maem*, and I'm going to
provide the food for tomorrow's funeral," Sue explained.
"I know what she wants, but is there anything special you
want me to bring?"

Rose shook her head. "*Nae denki*, I'm sure what *Maem*
requested is perfectly fine."

"And I'll be there, of course," Sue continued.

"*Denki*," Rose said again, politely. She wiped her mouth with her napkin and then set it next to her empty plate.

"And, Mrs. Troyer," Sue said excitedly, "It's so good to see you again! Are you here for the funeral?"

"Oh, *nae*, not originally," Beth responded, "Abigail and I had planned this visit some time ago." She continued, "But I will be attending the ceremony, and I will head home the next morning."

"Ah, I see," Sue said, her hands clasped together in front of her. "Well, how is everything with Mrs. Miller?"

"Very *gut, denki*," Beth answered. "She really wanted to join me, but I insisted on traveling alone to spend some time with Abigail on this visit. I promised she could ride along next time." Beth chuckled.

"Is the trip up here from Little Valley pretty easy then?" Sue asked.

"*Jah*, it's not bad. The Amish taxi is quite safe and convenient," Beth responded.

"You know, I heard someone else say the same thing just recently," Sue said, her eyes shifting to the left as she tried to remember. "There was a lady in here just a few days ago... you know, I think she said she was from Little Valley, too."

Abigail quickly glanced at her mother, and Beth looked at Abigail, her left eyebrow raised.

Sue continued, "It's weird. I think she said she was here on business. I can't remember her name now."

"Was it Eliza Mayer?" Beth asked pointedly.

Sue snapped her fingers and pointed at Beth. "That's it! That's exactly it! Do you know her?"

Abigail, Beth and Rose all exchanged shocked looks, one by one.

I can't believe it, Abigail thought to herself. *Could her mother be right about this?*

Chapter Twelve

"We need to tell Chief Edwards," Beth insisted, as they climbed into the buggy.

"*Jah*, I agree, we do. And we will," Abigail said. "But, while we're over here, can I run into the craft store? I need to pick up some yarn for my crochet. I promise I'll be quick."

Rose and Beth agreed, and Rose directed her horse down Main Street toward the Billingsley Craft Store, parking in one of the only empty spaces in front of the building. Beth and Rose decided to wait for Abigail outside in the buggy since Abigail promised she would be quick.

Walking into the store, Abigail inhaled a deep breath. She loved the smell of wood mixed with fabric and yarn and craft paint. There was something about it that energized her. She had been in the store several times and she knew exactly what she needed, so she made a beeline for aisle twelve where the yarn is shelved.

She took a few minutes to select the colors she needed to complete the order of tiny owls that had become so popular at the gift store which sold her finished goods. With the new skeins in hand, she headed toward the cashiers and stood in line behind a lady she didn't know.

The lady looked a few years younger than Abigail. She was well dressed, wearing pressed slacks, high heels, and a beautiful light jacket that looked hand tailored. Abigail admired the craftsmanship of the jacket. It reminded her of something her cousin Sarah would sew on special request for Englischers. It fit her like a glove. And standing behind her, Abigail's eyes were drawn to the cuffs of the jacket. The ladies' left hand was down by her side and shiny petite gold buttons with hearts engraved in the center immediately caught Abigail's eye.

The next customer in line was called to the register and everyone else in line moved forward a few steps, making the woman with the beautiful jacket the first in line. Only then did Abigail catch the attention of the well-dressed lady in front of her, and the woman's reaction was not a pleasant one. She stared at Abigail, her eyes cold and angry, and took another short step to put some extra inches between herself and Abigail.

Abigail had witnessed this sort of behavior before. She was aware that not everyone approved of the Amish lifestyle and knew to just keep her distance. She smiled warmly, but the woman in front of her scoffed and wrinkled her nose, looking away. She turned her back to Abigail once again and shifted her basket of merchandise to her left hand, letting her right hand drop to her side.

Abigail's attention to detail drew her eyes to the cuff of her right sleeve and immediately noticed there was a button missing on that cuff, right before the woman was called to the register. Expressing an exaggerated sigh of relief, the woman scurried to the register, glancing over her shoulder at Abigail as if she was worried Abigail would follow her.

When she stepped up to the counter, the cashier greeted her by name. "Hello, Mrs. Nichols, how are you today?"

Mrs. Nichols responded, "Well, I could be better." She glanced back at Abigail and muttered something under her breath to the cashier.

The cashier looked at Abigail apologetically and ignored whatever Mrs. Nichols muttered.

"Did you find everything you were looking for?" she asked.

"No," Mrs. Nichols responded, her tone short and irritable. "I'm looking for a button for my jacket. I lost it when I traveled to Morocco recently, and you don't have anything like it." She showed the cashier the button, and the cashier assured her that it was a custom made button that she had never seen the store stock before. She promised to leave the manager a note to see if she could order something similar and would be in touch.

Mrs. Nichols seemed satisfied with that answer, paid for the items in her basket and exited out the front door.

The same cashier called Abigail over next, and apologized for how Mrs. Nichols acted.

"Oh, thank you, but that's not necessary," Abigail responded kindly. "I am not harmed in any way," she assured the friendly cashier, "and I'll definitely be back to visit your wonderful store again." The two chatted about the increasing prices of yarn as she paid for her order, and Abigail headed outside to join her mother and Rose.

She had already forgotten about the lady in the beautiful jacket by the time she climbed into the buggy.

Chapter Thirteen

Abigail, Jeremiah, Jo, Emma, and Beth all walked together to the ceremony building in the center of the community to attend Charlotte's funeral. The sky was clear and the temps were a bit cooler than they had been the previous few days, which seemed to sort of set the mood.

After the ceremony, Jeremiah joined the men's circle. Abigail noticed that Adam looked clean and content, and seemed a bit more relaxed than when he had his blow-up at the previous dinner. She wondered what ever came of the house search and the further investigation that the police were planning.

The kids ran off to play with their friends, while Abigail and Beth stayed close to Rose and Gracie, making sure they had full cups of tea, snacks, and whatever else they needed.

Abigail thought the funeral and burial ceremony seemed to provide a sense of closure for Rose. She looked relieved and almost renewed when the burial was concluded and the last of the attendees showed their respect and gave praise to *Gotte*.

"That was a nice ceremony, wasn't it?" Abigail's mother asked when they were headed back home, Jo and Emma in tow.

"*Jah*, I thought it was nice," Abigail answered. "I can't honestly say I've been to many funerals in my lifetime, and I'm always surprised at how much peace they bring to the family."

"I agree," Jeremiah chimed in. "There is a sense of closure in the air, for sure. Adam seemed much more at ease today than even a couple days ago."

"Same with Rose and Gracie," Abigail said. "I noticed the same with them."

"*Vell*, let's just hope there are no more murders taking place around here. The town of Billingsley needs a break," Beth said, and both Jeremiah and Abigail agreed emphatically.

"I'm sad you're leaving tomorrow, *Maem*," Abigail said, linking arms with her mother. "This has been such a nice visit."

"Indeed, I am sad to leave," Beth said, "But I miss your *dat* and Aunt Anna and everyone else. You all must plan a visit down to Little Valley before too long."

As the family approached their house, a short police siren could be heard behind them, causing them to stop in their tracks and turn to look. Most of the community was outside, lined up along the streets, watching as Chief Edwards' patrol car pulled up at Adam and Charlotte's house.

"Oh, no," Abigail said, under her breath. Beth shuffled Jo and Emma into the house, shielding them from witnessing the scene that was about to unfold. Several other mothers did the same with their children. The rest of the community watched silently as Chief Edwards and Officer Singer approached Adam's house. He opened the door before they could knock and stood there, his head hung, his eyes on the ground. He cooperated as they told him to hold his hands out in front of him and then slipped handcuffs on him before guiding him out to the car.

The crowd watched as they guided him past Gracie and Rose. Rose had her arms around Gracie as she cried loudly on her shoulder. Rose's children tugged at her dress, asking what was happening. Rose pointed toward the house, muttering something to the children, and Abigail watched as Jeb corralled them inside.

Officer Singer opened the back door of the patrol car and Adam slipped inside, his eyes still cast downward. No one else spoke a word. All eyes were on the taillights of the patrol car as it drove slowly up Burnt Hill Road to the highway.

Abigail caught Rose's eyes from several yards away, and watched as the previous relief and renewal that she had seen on Rose's face just minutes before faded away.

Jeremiah reached out and wrapped his arm around her shoulders, guiding her gently into the house. Abigail felt helpless. This was not the ending anyone had hoped for.

Chapter Fourteen

A bigail filled the watering can for the third time and made another round, touching the dirt in each pot to see which potted plants were thirsty. She glanced over at Angel who seemed comfortable enough on her bed at the end of the counter. Abigail still had a lot to learn about running a flower shop, but she didn't mind it at all so far. Of course, it was only her second day and the town of Billingsley was still getting used to Blooms and More reopening after being closed for a week.

The first day, Abigail experienced a few customers coming in to see where the murder had taken place, which was a bit unsettling, but she assumed that strange interest would fade away with time. She just wasn't sure how long Rose would need her help at the shop.

Staying focused, next Abigail removed all the wilted flowers from their plastic vases and tossed them in a plastic bin to put out back in the compost pile. There weren't as many of those to remove since she had done a very thorough job the day before. She began carrying some of the prettier potted plants out to the front stoop, arranging them so that their best sides were facing the street and the different colors and plant varieties were mixed and interesting.

Just as she had set the last potted plant down, the door to the cigar shop opened and Mr. Goldy stepped outside.

"What are you doing here?" he asked, in the same abrupt manner he always spoke.

Abigail refrained from snapping and decided to try to kill the seemingly unhappy man with kindness instead.

"Good morning, Mr. Goldy," she said in her most chipper voice. "I'm just helping Rose Swarey out with reopening the shop."

Mr. Goldy grunted and then looked out at the sky across the street. It wasn't lost on Abigail that he didn't have a mean reply this time. She smiled and crossed her arms, standing and looking in the same direction as him.

"I heard about Charlotte's husband getting arrested," Mr. Goldy said, his eyes still focused forward.

"Oh, yes," Abigail responded. "That is true, I'm afraid."

Mr. Goldy glanced over at Abigail and then returned to his original stance before continuing. "Do y'all think he did it?"

Abigail could only assume that by "y'all," Mr. Goldy was referring to the Amish community, so she answered on their behalf, short and sweet.

"No, we don't think Adam is the killer."

Mr. Goldy grunted again, this time following the grunt with clearing his throat.

"You know, my shop being next to Charlotte's never bothered me," he said in his grisly-like voice.

Abigail thought that might be the closest thing to a compliment Mr. Goldy ever gave. She swallowed a smile, nodded and responded with "Mmhmm."

That answer seemed to satisfy Mr. Goldy. After a few moments, he excused himself and returned to his shop. Abigail felt like it was progress and couldn't wait to tell Rose about the conversation. Just as the thought crossed her mind, she caught a glimpse of Rose driving her horse and buggy up the street towards the store. She waved and watched as Rose parked and joined her inside.

She knew Rose had just visited Adam, and she was anxious to hear how he was.

"How'd it go?" Abigail asked, pouring Rose some water and setting the paper cup in front of her.

"Oh, it's so sad," Rose said. "He's not doing well at all, emotionally. He's just a mess."

"Ugh," Abigail said. "I can't imagine what it must be like, with all he's been through."

"*Jah*," Rose continued. "They are setting his bail this afternoon, and if he can post bail, he can come home until the trial."

"Any idea how much it will be?" Abigail asked.

"I'm afraid it will most likely be more than any of us in the community can afford, but we'll pray the judge has mercy on him and makes it affordable."

Abigail nodded.

"There's nothing we can do in the meantime," Rose added. "Did I miss anything? Did everything go alright with your *maem* catching the taxi this morning?" She settled onto the stool.

"*Jah, Maem* should be home by lunch. I miss her already," Abigail said solemnly.

Abigail was about to fill Rose in on the conversation with Mr. Goldy when a gentleman entered the shop. He was clean-cut, wearing a crisp button-down shirt and pressed slacks, and no jacket.

Rose jumped off the stool and welcomed him to Blooms and More. She introduced herself and then introduced Abigail next.

"Can we help you find anything?" Abigail asked.

The man approached the counter and said, "Yes, please. I would like to send some flowers to my mother at the nursing home on Fourth Avenue. I have a regular account here. I usually work with..." His voice trailed off and Abigail thought she saw a flicker of pain cross his eyes before he looked away, but she wondered if it was her imagination.

He took an interest in Angel instead.

"Oh, who do we have here?" he said, rubbing her ears with both hands. If Angel was a cat, she'd be purring, but instead, her tail wagged from side to side and her eyes were half-closed as the man bent down, petting her.

"That's Angel," Abigail said. "You just happen to be petting her exactly how she likes it," she chuckled. "You must have a dog at home?"

"Oh, no, my wife would never allow a dog in the house, and I couldn't bear to lock one outside," the man explained. "I grew up with dogs, though. They sure make wonderful companions."

He stood up and looked over at Rose.

"Are you related to the previous owner?" he asked. "You look a little bit like her."

Rose nodded. "Yes, Charlie... I mean, Charlotte... was my little sister."

The man forced a half smile and swallowed before quietly saying, "I'm so sorry for your loss. I truly am."

"Thank you," Rose responded kindly. "What was your name again?" she asked.

"Oh, forgive me," he said, clearing his throat. "My name is Joel Nichols. Like I said, I'm a regular customer. I send my mother a bouquet of flowers each week. I usually order them on Wednesdays, but, you know..." Again, his words trailed off as he referred to the tragedy that took place which shut the shop down for a few days.

Abigail thought she recognized the name, but she couldn't place it.

"Right, right." Rose interjected. "Well, let's see if we can't get you back on schedule. She picked up a pad of paper from the counter and asked, "What type of flowers do you want to send your mother?"

Mr. Nichols answered quickly, "Oh, I always send her gardenias."

Abigail stifled a gasp. Suddenly, everything was coming together in her mind. The extra inventory of gardenias, the mention that he was a regular customer, the way he spoke about Charlotte.

Could this be the Englischer whom Charlotte was developing feelings for?

Abigail glanced at Rose and was confident they were thinking the same thing.

Chapter Fifteen

After Mr. Nichols placed his order and left, Abigail and Rose were almost giddy with excitement over possibly deciphering who Charlotte had developed feelings for, but all that came to a quick halt when Abigail asked the most important question: "Wait, do you think Mr. Nichols would have killed Charlotte?"

Rose's smile disappeared and she shook her head. "No way," she said. "I really can't imagine that at all."

"I know," Abigail said. "There would be no motive, right?"

Rose and Abigail sat in silence for a few minutes, reeling from the experience, their minds both racing ninety miles an hour.

Angel started whining, and Abigail realized she probably needed to go outside.

"I'm going to take Angel on a quick walk," she told Rose. "We'll be right back, and we'll talk about it some more. No matter what, I feel like we're closer to finding the answer."

"I agree," Rose said. "I feel like we're missing something really obvious."

Abigail was bent down to put Angel's harness on when Angel went to do a full body shake. Shielding herself from the whip of Angel's ears, something caught Abigail's eye. On the floor, wedged under the counter was a shiny gold circular object.

"What is that?" Abigail said out loud, reaching to retrieve it. Pulling it out from under the counter, she recognized it instantly. It was a gold button with a heart engraved in the center of it. Her mouth dropped open, and she instantly remembered why the name Nichols sounded so familiar to her.

This button belonged to the Mrs. Nichols that was in line in front of Abigail at the craft store.

Mrs. Nichols had told the cashier that she lost it while on vacation in Morocco.

And the cashier told Mrs. Nichols that the button was custom made, not sold locally.

If Mr. Nichols was the one who came in all the time to order the flowers for his mother, why would Mrs. Nichols's lost button be wedged on the floor under the counter?

All of the pieces of the puzzle were coming together rapidly in Abigail's mind.

Is that why Mrs. Nichols was so rude at the craft store? Because she was Amish, and her husband had developed feelings for Charlotte?

Could she be the one who killed Charlotte?

"*Ach du lieva,* Rose," Abigail said, standing up slowly, holding the button out in the open palm of her hand. "I think I know who killed your sister."

Rose gasped, her eyes eager for the answer. Abigail filled her in on everything, and Rose threw her arms around Abigail giving her the biggest bear hug, while jumping up and down at the same time.

"We have to go tell Chief Edwards everything right now," she said, wringing her hands with excitement.

Chapter Sixteen

A bigail and Rose sat side by side on the top step of Abigail's front porch. The sun was shining and the weather was comfortably warm for an early Autumn day. Angel was switching back and forth from napping in the sun to rolling on her back in the thick green grass in the front yard.

Adam was due to be dropped off at home anytime now, and Chief Edwards promised the ladies a short visit while she was there. They were waiting, excited to hear the details of the case.

"I can't believe you found that button," Rose said, leaning back on her palms, her face lifted to the sun. She smiled and Abigail was happy to see her friend had finally found peace.

"I can't believe it either," Abigail said, chuckling. "Who knows how long it would have been there, wedged under the counter, if I hadn't bent down to get Angel ready for a walk."

"I know," Rose said, "and that lady would have possibly gotten away scot free with killing Charlie." She straightened her back, facing forward again, and shook her head. "I can't even allow myself to think about that," she said.

"Well, the beauty of it all is that you don't have to think about that anymore," Abigail said. "Mr. Goldy said that her arrest made the papers, and now we just wait for things to be cleared up in court for Adam this morning."

"And all will be right with the world again," Rose said. "Except, I'll forever miss my sister."

"*Jah*, Charlotte will forever be missed," Abigail said, "and remembered for the talented wonderful woman she was."

Rose nodded, swallowing hard, and Abigail gently touched her shoulder.

"It's a happy ending to a bad story," Rose said, pushing back her tears. "I'm still shocked that my little sister had developed feelings for an *Englischer*."

"Well, he did seem pretty special," Abigail said, nudging Rose with her elbow, and chuckling. "I'm teasing, of course."

Rose laughed and said, "Well, it's true."

"You know, in a weird way, Adam is kind of a hero in this whole thing, too. Turns out Charlotte was a lucky girl. They say that only true love covers a multitude of sins, and that's what Adam was trying to do. He was trying to protect his wife from all the judgment she would get for her truths," Abigail explained.

"*Jah*, that's exactly right," Rose said. "And Charlotte should get some credit for being honest enough to tell Adam about her feelings. Even though it may appear selfish from an outside perspective, she did the right thing to confide in her husband and share the truth about her temptations. It's honestly more than some women would do."

"Oh, absolutely," Abigail agreed. "Absolutely."

"There they are!" Rose said, jumping to her feet when she saw the patrol car headed down the hill. The two friends ran up the road to meet Chief Edwards and welcome Adam home. The car parked in front of Adam's house and he almost leapt out of the passenger side of the car before it came to a full stop, a broad grin on his face.

"*Vilkumme* home, brother!" Rose said, running up and throwing her arms around him.

"*Denki*!" he exclaimed. "I'm so glad to be home!"

"Hi, Chief!" Abigail greeted Chief Edwards as she stepped out of the car.

"Hello!" she responded, cheerily. "Boy, I sure am glad to be bringing this guy home to you ladies today!" She wore a grin on her face almost as big as Adam's. "All of us at the station just knew he was innocent from the beginning."

Adam blushed. "Well, if it wasn't for you two, I don't know if I would still be standing here right now."

Abigail and Rose looked at each other and smiled.

"I just can't thank you enough," Adam said. "I will be forever in your debt. Both of you."

"*Nae*," Abigail said, waving her hand in the air. "That's not necessary. We just want you to be happy and take care of yourself."

"Exactly," Rose said. "That's exactly what Charlie would say if she were here with us."

"Speaking of Charlotte," Chief Edwards continued. "You'll be happy to hear that Mrs. Nichols made a full confession this morning."

Abigail and Rose gasped in unison, their mouths open. Rose reached out and grabbed Abigail's hand and squeezed it.

"Really?" Abigail asked. "What did she say?"

"Well," Chief Edwards continued, "at first, she started to say that she had never been in the flower shop. But then, all I had to do was pull out the button you had found. Once she saw that, she got scared and confessed everything. She showed up right before the shop closed that night, held Charlotte at gunpoint, and shot her dead."

Rose still held Abigail's hand, and this time Abigail squeezed hers, glancing over to make sure she was okay.

"Why would she do that?" Adam asked the question that everyone needed to hear.

"It was jealousy, as she tells it," the chief continued. "Her husband confessed that he had developed an innocent crush for Charlotte, and she just flipped out. She said she didn't want anyone to know. She said she couldn't bear the thought of Mr. Nichols ever acting on it or the chance of a relationship blooming."

The four of them stood quietly for a moment. Abigail, Rose and Adam soaked in everything the chief was telling them.

Abigail broke the silence. "Did she really use that word, *blooming*?" she asked with a mischievous grin.

Chief Edwards smiled and chuckled. "Yep, she really did."

The four of them burst into laughter at the irony of it all, and Abigail took a moment in between breaths to be present and just enjoy the sound of laughter replacing all the tears from the previous week.

Rose's husband, Jeb, came out of their house to greet Adam with a pat on the back and the three of them fell into conversation of their own while Abigail walked Chief Edwards back to her patrol car.

"Well, you did it again, Abigail," the chief said. "I'm starting to think I need you on the force."

"Oh, no," Abigail chuckled. "I am not cut out for all that," she said.

"I don't know how you do it," Chief Edwards said. "What's the secret to being such a talented amateur detective, can you tell me?" She winked.

Abigail shrugged, with a grin. "I think it's in my blood. I've learned everything I know from my mother and my aunt."

"Ah, that makes sense," the chief said.

"Oh," Abigail added, "and maybe a little bit is from reading a fair share of mystery books."

"I'll give that a try then," Chief Edwards said before she loaded into her car and pulled away, waving to everyone as she disappeared up the hill and turned onto the highway out of sight.

Want more mystery from The Abigail Baker Mystery Series? Check out the mystery that started it all in the prequel to this series, Blind Faith.Grab your copy at **marybbarb ee.com/blindfaith**.

Want to read more Amish mystery with a surprising twist? Find *The Amish Lantern Mystery Series* on marybbarbee .com, and get started reading today!

A Note from the Author

This may have been one of the most difficult stories I have written. As an Amish mystery writer, it is certainly not easy to create a scenario where the murder victim is Amish, let alone having unclean thoughts. But I am very happy how the story came together so beautifully, proving that even the most devout are not perfect... and are still loved by many.

I tend to gravitate toward writing a story where there is a special bond between sisters, and this came to light again with Rose and Charlotte's relationship. The sisters were so close despite several years difference in age. There were definitely tears shed as I wrote some of the scenes where Rose was grieving, and I honestly fell in love with Rose's character even a bit more, as a result.

I thoroughly enjoyed bringing Beth and her quirky sense of humor and genuine kindness back into this story, with a short visit from Little Valley to Billingsley. Abigail misses her mother terribly in her new town, and the mother and daughter are so similar as amateur detectives – it's just so easy to write the scenes that include the two of them together.

And sweet Angel also has a special place in my heart. I am a dog lover myself, and I'm convinced now that every future main character must be the same.

Thank you for choosing *A Multitude of Sins* to add to your collection!

And if you haven't already read the books in *The Amish Lantern Mystery Series*, it's not too late! The main characters are Beth and her twin sister, Anna, and they work together to solve a crime in each book in the series. And just as with *The Abigail Baker Mystery Series*, you can start anywhere in the series without feeling like you missed something important in the previous book.

Happy Reading!

With so much gratitude,
Mary B. Barbee

About the Author

Mary B. Barbee is the author of *The Amish Lantern Mystery Series* and *The Abigail Baker Mystery Series*. As an avid fan of all mystery and suspense in print, on television and in film, Mary B. believes the best mystery is one where the suspect changes throughout the story, keeping the audience guessing. She enjoys providing an exciting escape for a few hours with stories her readers can't put down - and always with a surprise ending.

When not writing, Mary B. is either playing a couple sets of tennis or a strategy board game with her two witty daughters and her kindly competitive mother. The four of them share a home in the Inland Northwest in the beautiful town of Spokane, Washington with their really cute - but sometimes naughty - chihuahua.

Mary loves to hear from her readers. Connect at:
marybbarbee@gmail.com
www.facebook.com/marybbarbee
Instagram: @marybbarbee
www.marybbarbee.com

More Books to Read By Mary B. Barbee

THE AMISH LANTERN MYSTERY SERIES

Thick As Thieves – Book 1

Robberies are running rampant in Little Valley, and the quiet small-town lives of the Amish community are suddenly thrown into chaos.

Secrets in Little Valley – Book 2

With the bishop's daughter suddenly missing and a new sheriff in town, Anna and Beth find themselves roped into solving another mystery in their small town.

Saving Grace – Book 3

The Amish community in Little Valley is facing big changes, and big threats, with tourism booming. It becomes clear that some of the new businesses want control of the market, and it looks like they are willing to go to great lengths to get it.

Good Intentions – Book 4

Hazel Thompson is found dead in Little Valley's now-famous Amish Inn, and there's a long list of suspects with plenty of motive.

A Blessing in Disguise – Book 5

Jessica McLean opens shop to find a man has been left for dead on the floor of her diner. Could the crime could be related to Jessica's new relationship with their beloved Matthew Beiler?

Christmas Chaos in Little Valley - Book 6

Beth finds out that the Little Valley library is shutting its doors due to a lack of funding and very disturbing anonymous threats.

THE ABIGAIL BAKER MYSTERY SERIES
Blind Faith – Prequel
Abigail's excitement for her new home is replaced by doom and gloom when she finds out that an unexplained murder has rocked the residents of her new town. And not unusual to her, it's the Amish community that is suspect number one.

Grab your free e-copy of Blind Faith at:
marybbarbee.com/blindfaith

Where Fear Ends – Book 1
A town councilman is found dead by the side of the road in the Amish community of Abigail Baker's new hometown.

A Multitude of Sins – Book 2

When secret notes containing serious threats are unveiled, Abigail wonders if the latest victim could have been hiding a multitude of sins.

A Wing and a Prayer – Book 3 ~ COMING SOON!

THE PUPCAKE MYSTERY SERIES
Cupcakes and Corruption – Prequel

Battling empty-nest syndrome, Eliza finds solace in the company of her adorable chihuahua, Pupcake, and her dreams of opening a quaint coffee shop. Little does she know that her talent for baking and nurturing also extends to amateur sleuthing.

Grab your free e-copy of Cupcakes and Corruption at:
marybbarbee.com/pupcakeprequel

Sweet Suspicion – Book 1

The charming town of Copeland is buzzing with excitement as Eliza and her adorable chihuahua, Pupcake, open their new coffee shop. But when a body is discovered on the premises, the duo must put down their baking tools and pick up their detective hats.

Confections and Clues – Book 2 – Coming Valentine's Day 2025

Eliza and Pupcake's lakeside getaway takes a dark turn when they stumble upon a body. With a secretive small town and a case no one wants solved, Eliza's sweet retreat quickly turns into another mystery. Can she and Pupcake crack the case before the killer's trail goes cold?

Recipe for Reckoning – Book 3 ~ COMING SOON!

———◄○►———

Find excerpts, purchase links and more at
www.marybbarbee.com